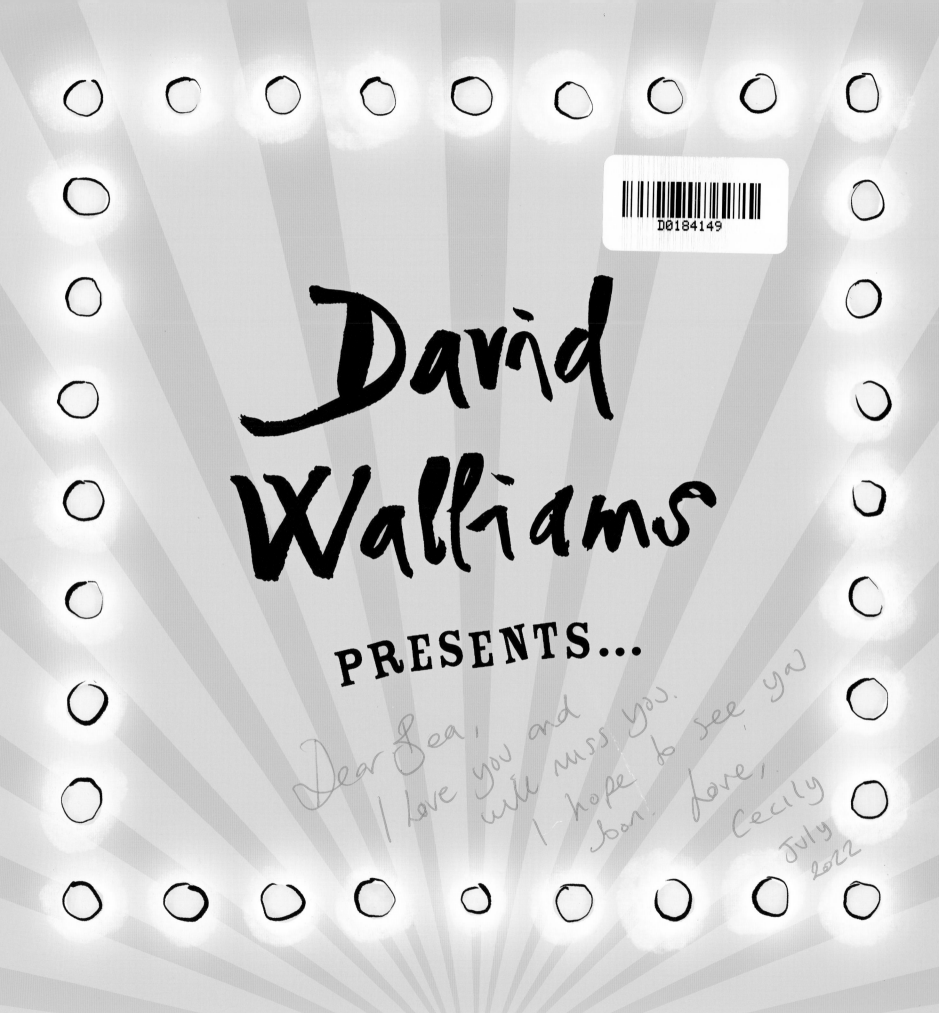

David Walliams

PRESENTS...

Dear Bea,
I love you and
will miss you.
I hope to see ya
soon. Love,
Cecily
July
2022

For Max Valentine.

With all my love,

Uncle David x

To wonderful Nelly and Ted.

T.R.

First published in hardback in the United Kingdom by HarperCollins *Children's Books* in 2019
Published in this paperback edition in 2022

HarperCollins *Children's Books* is a division of HarperCollins*Publishers* Ltd
1 London Bridge Street, London SE1 9GF

www.harpercollins.co.uk

HarperCollins*Publishers* Ltd
1st Floor, Watermarque Building, Ringsend Road,
Dublin 4, Ireland

1 3 5 7 9 10 8 6 4 2

ISBN: 978-0-00-854195-8

Printed and bound in Italy

Illustrated by the artistic genius

Tony Ross

THE CREATURE CHOIR

HarperCollins *Children's Books*

Warble was a **walrus** who loved to **warble**.

She **warbled** on the ice.

"Bom! Bom! Bom!"

She **warbled** underwater.

"Blub! Blub! Blub!"

She warbled **all** day and **all** night.

Warble's dream was to warble all over the world.
And maybe one day even take part in

..... THE .....
★ ✦ ★ GREAT BIG ANIMAL TALENT SHOW. ★

There was just ONE teeny-weeny problem.
The sound she made was absolutely . . .

. . . shocking!

Whenever Warble warbled,
seals scarpered . . .

Plop!

. . . bears bolted . . .

Dash!

. . . and puffins pegged it.

Flutter!

The huddle couldn't take any more.
The biggest, fattest one bellowed,

"No more warbling, Warble!"

"But—" she pleaded.

"No buts! When you warble, Warble, it is awful!"

"But warbling makes me happy.
Please can I warble some more?"

"Noooo!"

The whole huddle joined in the chorus of "no"s, except **one.**
Warble's friend, the littlest walrus, stuck up for her.

"*No!*"

"*No!*"

"*No!*"

"But Warble **loves** to warble. She lives to warble! Warble **must** warble!"

Not warbling made Warble **sad.**

One morning, the sun was shining and Warble just couldn't help herself. Warble warbled like **never** before.

"Bom! Bom! Bom! Bom!"

Warble warbled so loudly she caused an avalanche!

Whoosh!

Everybody was buried in deep, deep snow.

The avalanche was the final straw. That night, while Warble was warbling in her sleep, the huddle made their **escape!**

"No one make a sound!" hissed the biggest, fattest one. "Now follow me!"

"Where on earth are we going?" asked the littlest one.

"As far away from Warble as we can go! The Antarctic!"

"But—"

"Son, I said, 'Follow me!'"

They all tip-flippered across the ice, and one by one plopped into the water.

Plop! Plop! Plop!

The littlest one took a last look at his friend . . .

"Never stop warbling, Warble."

. . . before disappearing off into the inky sea.

When Warble woke up
the next morning, she
was **all alone**
on the ice.

"Hello?"

she called out sorrowfully.
"Is anybody there?"

Silence.

Now all she had to keep her
company was her **warble**.
So Warble warbled.

"Bom!
Bom!
Bom!"

Her warble was heard miles away by a moose.
He too was all alone, having been abandoned by his herd for his

monstrous mooing.

On hearing Warble's warble, he began to moo.

"Moo! Moo! Moo!"

He galloped across the ice to find her.
They sang their hearts out.

"Bom! Bom!" "Moo!" "Bom! Bom!" "Moo!"

This duet was heard miles away by **another** lonely creature.

A snorting **snow hare.**

"Oh my goodness, they sound even more horrendous than me!" she snorted.

"Snort! Snort! Snort!"

The snow hare's thunderous snorts had sent her drove of hares fleeing.

She bounced towards
the pair to join them. "Bom!" "Moo!" "Snort!"

they sang together.

They were now
A TRIO!

But not for long.

Soon, so **many** creatures
joined them that . . .

...it was **a choir.**

THE CREATURE CHOIR

"Bark!"

"Moo!"

"Snort!"

"Bom!"

All animals were welcome.
Warble never, ever said no to **anybody.**

The sound the Creature Choir made was nothing short of . . .

atrocious!

"Quack!" "Hoot!" "Roar!" "Honk!"

"Hee-haw!"

But their joy when they sang together was a thing of **wonder.**
The smiles on their faces could **light up** all the dark.

Just as Warble had dreamed, her choir began performing **all over the world.**

They sang in forests, where they **toppled** tall trees.

Donk!

They sang on mountaintops, triggering thunder and lightning.

Kaboom!

And they sang in deserts, starting **sandstorms.**

Whoosh!

"Bom!" "Moo!" "Snort!" "Bark!"

"Roar!" "Hee-haw!" "Hoot!" "Quack!"

"Honk!" "Buzz!"

"Trumpet!"

"Chirp!"

Still the choir grew
bigger and **bigger** and **bigger.**

The Creature Choir sang all around the world.
Now Warble thought they were ready for

..... THE .....
★ ☆ GREAT BIG ANIMAL TALENT SHOW. ★
☆ ☆

This year, it was happening at the Antarctic.
On the day the choir arrived for the competition,
all the creatures became n-n-n-nervous.

They only sang for the joy of it, not because
they thought they were the BEST.

They knew they were the WORST.

So they looked on with trepidation
as an elephant seal sang **opera**,

and a king penguin delighted
all the animals with a selection of

show tunes.

Finally, it was the Creature Choir's turn.
Warble calmed everyone's nerves by telling them:

"Don't worry about being good or bad –
just sing and be happy!"

They all nodded, and began . . .

The smiles on their faces **delighted** everyone,
even if the noise they made was . . .

...which swept the audience of animals **off** the ice.

Splosh!

Among those clambering back on, Warble spotted some familiar, if wet, faces – her huddle of **walruses**.

When the Creature Choir finally finished their song, there was **silence**.

Then the littlest walrus began **clapping,**

The whole crowd went **wild.**

before all the walruses rose to their flippers
and burst into wild applause.

Flip! Flap! Flop!

There was no question about it. The Creature Choir were the winners of

THE
GREAT BIG ANIMAL TALENT SHOW.

"Hooray!"

"We've so missed you and your warbling, Warble," said the littlest one.

"I am sorry we left you all alone," said the biggest, **fattest** one, a tear welling in his eye. "Please can **we** join your Creature Choir?"

The **whole** huddle smiled hopefully, and all eyes turned to Warble.

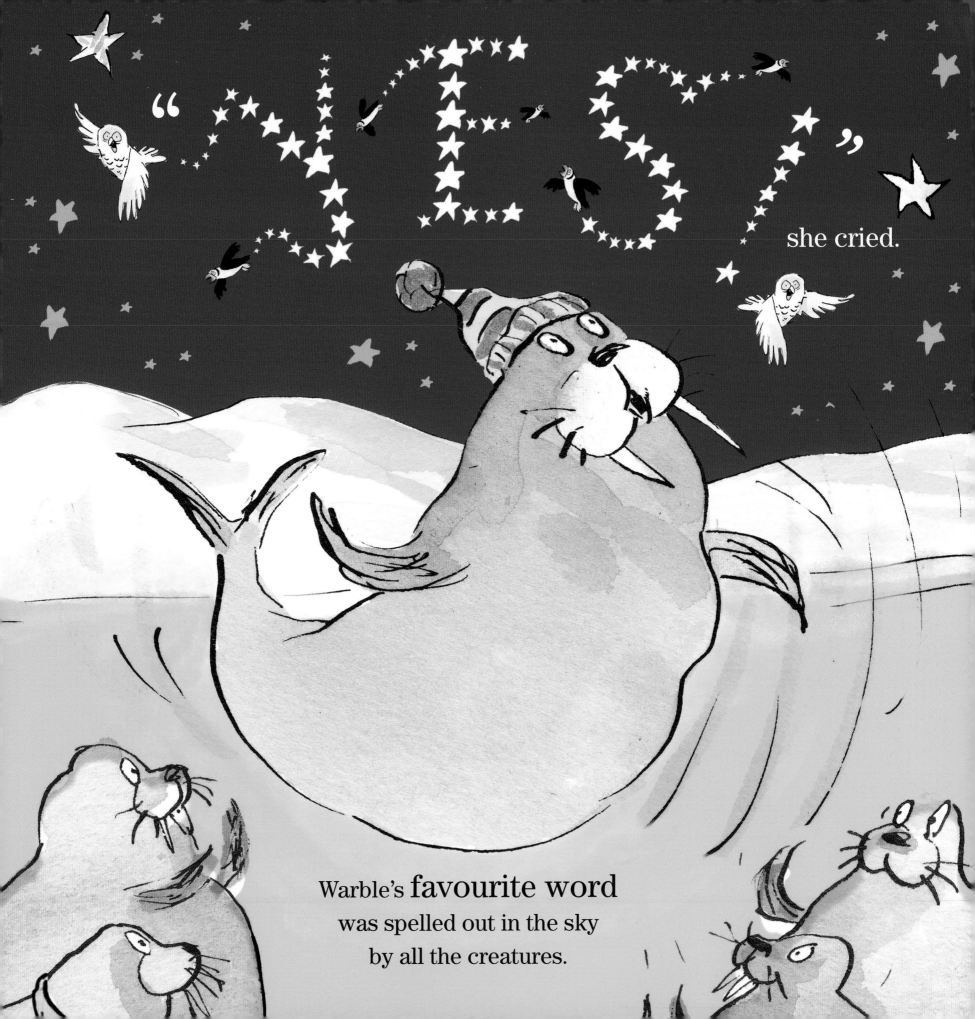

"YES?" she cried.

Warble's **favourite word**
was spelled out in the sky
by all the creatures.

All the other walruses warbled **worse** than Warble.

No matter.

All that **did** matter was that they were . . .